Isabel Butler

Our lady's tumbler

A tale of mediaeval France

Isabel Butler

Our lady's tumbler
A tale of mediaeval France

ISBN/EAN: 9783337120641

Printed in Europe, USA, Canada, Australia, Japan

Cover: Foto ©Andreas Hilbeck / pixelio.de

More available books at **www.hansebooks.com**

OUR LADY'S TUMBLER:
A TALE OF MEDIÆVAL
FRANCE & TRANSLATED
INTO ENGLISH FROM
THE OLD FRENCH BY
ISABEL BUTLER & BOS-
TON: COPELAND AND
DAY: MDCCCXCVIII

TRANSLATOR'S NOTE

OUR LADY'S TUMBLER is one of a large body of stories much beloved in Mediæval France that turn upon some miracle performed by the Virgin,—a type of story of which the most familiar example in English is the tale told by Chaucer's prioress. Early in the thirteenth century several collections of these miracles were compiled, the two most important being those of Gautier de Coinci, prior of Vic-Sur-Aisne, and of Jean le Marchant, a priest of Chatres. Though most of the legends are interesting to us to-day mainly for the curious insight they give us into the religious sentiment of the time, there are yet not a few that we like for their own sakes, for their naïveté, sincerity, and pathos.

These tales — of which about a hundred distinct examples remain, besides endless variations — differ much among themselves in incident and dramatis personæ. In them we are not, as in the romances, always in the company that Aucassin preferred, that "of the goodly clerks, and the goodly knights that fight in tourneys and great wars, and stout men of arms, and all men noble." Village priests and thieves and strolling mountebanks figure as heroes as well as knights and great lords.

One tale is of a poor priest, very devout, very charitable, and very ignorant. Being unable to read his breviary, he celebrated day after day the Mass of Our Lady, the only one that he knew by heart. At length news of the matter reached the bishop, who, much scandalised, straightway turned the offender out of office. But his disgrace was short, for that same night Our Lady appeared in a vision to the bishop and commanded that the good man be at once reinstated. Another story is of a thief who, however busy he might be about his trade, never forgot his prayers to the Virgin. And when at last he was taken and condemned to be hung, Our Lady herself stretched out her fair white hands beneath his feet and supported him, so that he felt no hurt or inconvenience from the rope about his neck. Those who had previously condemned now gladly released him; on thus regaining his freedom he entered a monastery and vowed himself to the service of the Virgin.

In spite of their variety of detail, all the stories are yet dominated by one common sentiment, —that of pity. It is true that from the point of view of justice this compassion seems often somewhat oddly bestowed, and the reward, say of the thief for duly reciting his prayers at proper intervals, wholly undeserved. Yet even such cases as these may be taken as but the extreme expression of the idea of human weakness and the power of forgiveness so deeply rooted in mediæval Christianity.

Though Our Lady's Tumbler shows this same spirit of naïve faith and devotion, it yet differs from the majority of similar tales by its subtler moral thinking, and a more lifelike presentment of its story. The minstrel himself, his embarrassment among his new companions, his doubts, his compunctions, his final determination to serve by his own trade as best he may, and the eagerness with which he goes about his work, all this comes home to us sharply enough. So too does the monk who spied upon the convert when at his curious devotions, and who could laugh at the spectacle and yet like the man the better for the earnestness with which he plied his trade. Thus instead of being hurried on to the miracle at the end, we are allowed to linger by the way; and through all the story we find something of the temper of the monk who was moved by the tumbler's way of serving both to mirth and to compassion.

The original, like most mediæval stories, is written in verse, the form being the much-used short octosyllabic line arranged in rhyming couplets. Of the history of the little poem we know almost nothing. Its editor, Wilhelm Fœrster, tells us that its language is of the end of the twelfth century, and its dialect that of the Isle de France. Beyond this his information is purely negative. Its author is unknown, and so too is its precise date; it is not found in any of the chief collections of the miracles of Our Lady, and, although its author asserts that he has found his material in the lives of the Fathers, its sources have not yet been discovered.

The poem, edited from a manuscript in the Arsenal Library in Paris, by Fœrster, first appeared in the "Romania" for 1873. It has, somewhat oddly, never been reprinted; so that the story that a specialist like M. Gaston Paris and a literary wanderer like M. Anatole France unite in praising is still only to be found in the back number of a learned magazine. In 1894 a translation by P. H. Wicksteed was published in England. The fact that the edition was a small one, and the book already out of print, excuses another version.

When Fœrster brought out the story in 1873, he knew of the existence of but a single manuscript. Since then two more have been found, a second in the Arsenal Library and another in the Na-

tional Library. In 1880 Gustav
Grœber published the variants of
these manuscripts in the " Zeit-
schrift für Romanische philolo-
gie " (Vol. IV.). The variations
of text are for the most part
slight and, from a literary point
of view, unimportant. In a few
instances, however, Grœber's
readings have been adopted in
the present translation.

OUR LADY'S TUMBLER

IN the lives of the early fathers, where there is much goodly matter, we are told this tale. I do not say that there is not many another to be heard fairer than this, only that this is not of so little worth but that it is good to tell. Now speak we of a certain minstrel and what befell him.

HE came and went for so long in divers places, and so wasted his strength, that at last, weary of the world, he withdrew into a holy order. His horses, his garments, his money, and all that he had he put therein, and left the world, for he would follow its ways no more. Thus,

1

then, he came into the monastery which, men say, was that
of Clairvaux. Now, though the
youth was of much worship, and
fair and well made and goodly,
he yet knew no craft of which
the folk there stood in any need.
For he had lived only by tumbling and leaping and dancing;
and though he knew right well
how to leap and to spring, he
knew naught beside, for no other
lesson had he ever learned, nor
knew he either Pater Noster, or
chant, or Credo, or Ave, or aught
else that might work for his sal-
vation.

NOW, when he was come
into the monastery and saw
the tonsured brethren who let

2

no word fall from their lips, but spoke among themselves by signs, he believed that they held communication one with another only in this wise. But soon he was undeceived, and learned that they denied themselves speech only as a penance, wherefore at certain times they were silent. And it seemed to him fitting that he too should forego speech; and he remained silent so cheerfully and so persistently that he would not speak for a whole day, were he not otherwise commanded, whereat there was often much laughter. And the minstrel was much abashed and ill at ease among the brethren, for he knew not how to share

3

by word or by deed in that which was the practice of the place; so was he dejected and heavy at heart. He saw the monks and the lay brothers each serving God in his place and after the manner appointed to him. He saw the priests before the altar, for that was their office; he saw the deacons at the Gospels, and the sub-deacons at the vigils; and the acolytes in their turn were ready at the Epistles when the time was. One recited a psalm, and another the lesson for the day; the young clerks were at their psalters, and the lay brothers at the litanies,— for such is the order in these matters,— while the more ignorant said their Pater Nosters.

4

E looked about him up and down through all the offices and courts, and in many a hidden corner he saw men in fours or fives or twos, or singly maybe; and if so that he might, he looked hard at every man of them. He heard one groan, and another weep, and a third sigh and lament, and much he marvelled what the matter might be. "Holy Mary," said he, "what is amiss with these men that they bear themselves thus, and make such dole? Methinks they must be sore vexed and troubled to bemoan themselves thus." Then he said again: "Holy Mary, alas, and woe is me! what is this that I have said? I do believe that

5

they pray God's mercy. But I, poor wretch that I am, what do I do here? There is no one so base in all the convent but strives to serve God in his own manner; but I have no trade that is of service to me here, and I do naught by word or by deed. Caitiff was I when I came into this place, for I know nor prayer, nor aught else that is good. I see one here and another there; but I do naught but dream away my time, and eat my bread to no purpose. Now, if this thing be noted concerning me, a sorry fall shall be mine, for they will cast me out of doors. And here am I a strong fellow, and yet I do naught but eat. Truly a poor creature am I

in a goodly place." Then he wept
to relieve his grief, and wished
he were dead. "Holy Mary,
Mother," he said again, "I beseech you pray God, your Sov-
ereign Father, that He hold me
in His favour, and that He send
me good counsel how I may
serve Him and you, and earn the
bread that I eat; for I know that
my present ways are evil."

WHEN he had bemoaned
himself thus, he went
away through the clois-
ter, looking this way and that,
until he came into a crypt; there
he crouched down by an altar,
drawing himself as close to it as
he might. Above the altar was
a statue of Our Lady, the Holy

Mary, and he did not go astray when he came into that place; no, in sooth, for God, who directs His own, had guided his footsteps thither. Anon, when he heard the mass begin, he sprang up dismayed, "Ah! how am I brought to shame," he cried; "now everyone is saying his lesson, and I am as a tethered ox, for I do naught but browse, and I eat my bread to no purpose. Shall I serve neither by word nor by deed? By the Mother of God, I will; nor shall I win any blame thereby; I will do what I have been taught to do, and I will serve the Mother of God here in her monastery by my own trade; the others serve by singing, and I will serve by tumbling."

He took off his cloak and disrobed himself, and laid his garments beside the altar; but that he might not be wholly naked, he kept on a coat that was light and fine of texture; of little more weight was it than a shirt, and the rest of his body was left free. He girded and busked him, right well he girded his coat and made him ready. Then he turned to the image, and looked up at it very humbly: "Lady," said he, "into your care I commit me, body and soul. Gentle Lady, Sweet Queen, do not despise that which I know, for I would serve you in all good faith, and so God

9

may help me, without offence. I know not how to read or to sing, but right gladly will I show you my most chosen tricks of tumbling; and I will be as the young calf that skips and springs before his mother. Lady, who are never cruel to those who serve you faithfully, such as I am now am I wholly yours."

Then he began to leap and to spring, now up and now down, beginning first with small capers, and then leaping higher and higher. And then he went down on his knees before the image, and bowed before it, saying: "Most Sweet Queen, of your grace and your mercy despise not my service." Then again he leaped and tumbled, and, to make merry, he did the trick of Metz around his head. Anon he bowed before the image and worshipped her, and honoured her with all that he had. Then he did the French trick and the trick of Champagne, and next the Spanish trick, and the tricks they do in Brittany, and then the trick of Lorraine; and he did them all with great travail, and spared himself not at all. Thereafter he did the Romish trick, and putting his hands before his face, danced right featly and fairly, as he looked all humbly upon the image of the Mother of God. "Lady," he said, "this is good disport; and I do it for no

11

other save for you and for your Son before all, so God may help me, I do not. And I dare boast and maintain that I do not do this for my own pastime, but only to serve you, and to acquit myself; the others serve, and I serve. Lady, despise not your thrall, for I serve you for your delight. Lady, you are the highest joy, whoever reckons all the world." Then he tumbled with his feet in the air, and went and came on his two hands, touching the earth only with these; yet even while his feet were dancing the tears fell from his eyes. "Lady," he said, "I worship you with my heart and my body, my feet and my hands, for I know not how to

worship you in any other way.
Henceforth will I be your minstrel; and while the others of
the convent are chanting within,
I will come and tumble here
for your delight. Lady, you can
guide me. In God's name, despise me not." Then he confessed his sins, and made moan
and wept softly, for that he knew
no other manner of worship.
Then he turned away and made
a spring. "Lady," he said, "so
God may save me, this thing
did I never before. This trick is
wholly new, and is not for common folk. Lady, how his desires
would be fulfilled who should
dwell with you in your glorious
manor. In God's name, Lady,

receive me there; wholly yours am I, nor mine at all." And again he did the trick of Metz, and tumbled and danced persistently. And when he heard the sound of the chant rise higher, he exerted himself the more; and as long as the mass lasted, so long did he leap and skip and dance, and never ceased till he was so spent that he could no longer hold himself upright, but sank down for very weariness, and fell to the ground exhausted; and as the fat runs out of a piece of roast meat, so the sweat ran off all his body from head to foot. "Lady," said he, "I can do no more now, but in sooth I will come again."

ALL burning seemed he with heat. He put on his garments, and when he had clothed himself he arose, and bowed before the image, and went his way. "Farewell," he said, "Most Sweet Friend, in God's name be not cast down, for if I may I will return, and every hour I will serve you the best I can,—if it please you, and if it be permitted to me." Then he went away, still looking back at the image. "Lady," said he, "much it repenteth me that I do not know all those psalters, for right gladly would I say them over for love of you, Most Sweet Lady. To you I commend me, body and soul."

15

AND he continued long in this way of life, returning without fail at every hour to offer his homage and his service before the image. For his delight lay in this thing; and gladly he performed it, so that there was never a day when he was so weary that he would not yet do his best for the delight of the Mother of God; nor did he ever desire other pastime.

THEY of the house knew, no doubt, that he went every day to the crypt, but no one, save God, knew what he did there; and he would not for all the riches of the world that any one save the Lord God alone were aware of his employment.

For he feared that if they should know of it they would straightway drive him out from thence, and cast him back into the world that so teems with sin; and he had rather that he were dead than that sin should again sting him. But God, who read the intent of this good man, and all his compunctions, and knew for whose love he did this thing, willed that his deed should no longer be hid. Rather, the Lord willed and determined that the labour of His friend should be known and made manifest, for the sake of His Mother for whose delight he had wrought, and that all might see and know and understand that God refuses no one that comes to Him in love, whatsoever his estate may be, if he but love God and do right.

DO you think that God would have prized his service if it had been offered without love? Nay, not so, however much he had tumbled; but it was the man's love that the Lord held dear. Though you toil and travail, and watch and fast, and weep and sigh, and groan and pray; though you do penance, and go to mass and to matins, and pay what you owe, and give all that you have,—yet, if you love not the Lord God with your whole soul, all these things are thrown away, so that, in sooth, they shall avail not for

18

yoursalvation. For without love
and without pity all labour is as
naught. God asks not for gold
nor for silver, but only for love
in the hearts of His people. And
this man loved God unfeign-
ingly, and therefore his service
was sweet to the Lord.

THE good man continued
long in this way of life. I
cannot tell you how many
years he lived at peace, but at
length he was thrown into much
trouble. For a monk took note
of him, and blamed him much
in his heart in that he came
not to matins; and he marvelled
what became of him, and said
within himself that he would
never rest until he had discov-

ered what manner of man this was, and what was the service that he did, and how he earned his bread. Now the monk so followed him, and so watched and spied upon him, that he saw him perform all his tricks, even as I have told you. "By my faith," he said, "this man makes merry; he holds higher festival, it seems to me, than all the rest of us together. While the others are at prayer, or at work throughout the household, this man dances here as bravely as if he had a hundred marks of silver. Yet he does his task well, and pays us what he owes. And this is right enough,—we sing for him and he tumbles for us; we pay him

20

and he pays us; and if we weep, he makes us good return. I would that all the convent might see him as I do now, — even though the terms were I should fast for it until night. There is no one, I think, who could keep from laughter if he saw the eagerness of this poor wretch, and how he exerts himself in his tumbling, and how he strives much, and spares himself not at all. God makes of it a penance for him, since he does it with no ill intent; and, certes, for my part I think no harm of it, for he does it, as I deem, in all good faith according to his light, and because he would not be idle." And with his own eyes the monk saw how, at each hour of the day, the good man toiled and rested not; and he laughed much thereat and wept, for he was moved by it both to mirth and to compassion.

E went to the abbot and told the whole story as you have already heard it, and the abbot arose and said to the monk: "Now do not spread this abroad, but be silent, for by your vows I command you; and do you obey my commandment to speak of it to no one save to me. And we will go together to see this thing, and learn the truth of it. And we will pray to the Heavenly King, and to His most Sweet Mother, the

22

Radiant, the Beloved, that she in her gentleness beseech her Son, her Father, her Lord, that I may see this sight to-day, if it be His will; that God thereby may be the more beloved, and the good man be not blamed,—if He wills thus." Then they went all quietly to the crypt, and without mishap hid themselves in a nook hard by the altar, in such wise that the good man saw them not. And the abbot and monk watched all the convert's devotions, and the divers tricks that he performed, and all his leaping and dancing; and they saw how he bowed before the image, and how he skipped and sprang till his strength failed

him. For he so exerted himself
in his weariness that he might
no longer hold himself upright,
but fell to the ground exhausted.
So worn and spent was he with
his labours that the sweat ran
out from all his body down upon
the floor of the crypt. But pres-
ently, and in a little space, his
most Sweet Lady came to succour him, she whom he had
served so truly, gladly she came
at his need.

AND the abbot watched
and straightway saw a
Lady come down to him
from the vault, so glorious
that none was ever seen like to
her in loveliness or in richness
of adornment, for none so beau-

tiful was ever born. Her garments were rich with gold and
precious stones; and with her
came angels and archangels
from heaven, who came about
the minstrel and gave him com-
fort and consolation. And when
they were gathered about him
his heart was lightened. Then
they hastened to serve him, for
they longed to reward him for
the service that he had paid to
their Lady, that most Sweet
Wonder. And the sweet and gracious Queen held in her hands a
white napkin, and with it she
fanned her minstrel right gently
before the altar. The Lady, noble
and gentle, fanned his face, and
neck, and body to cool him;

25

gladly she succoured him, and gave herself wholly to the task. But the good man takes no heed of this, for he neither sees nor knows what goodly company is about him.

The holy angels do him great honour; but now they may stay with him no longer, and their Lady stays not, but makes the sign of the cross upon him, and turns away. The holy angels follow her, yet they find a wondrous delight in gazing back upon their comrade, and do but await the hour when God shall call him from this life and they may receive his soul. And this the abbot and his monk saw in very deed a good four times; for

it befell that at every hour the
Mother of God returned to aid
and to succour her servant, —
well knows she how to succour
her own. And the abbot was
much rejoiced thereat, for he
had been very desirous to get
at the truth of the matter.

AND now God had clearly
shown that the service the
poor man offered to Him
was pleasing in His sight. The
monk was all abashed, and his
anguish burned him as a fire.
" My lord," he said to the abbot,
"have mercy! this is a very holy
man that I see here. Now if I
have spoken any evil concerning him it is right that my body
suffer for it. So lay a penance

27

upon me, for, in sooth, this is a good man and a true. We have seen all this matter from end to end, and we can never be in any doubt concerning it." And the abbot said: "You speak truly, and God has made it plain that He loves him with a great love. Now I command you straightway, in virtue of obedience, and if you would not fall under sentence, that you speak to no one of what you have seen, save only to God and to me." "My lord," he said, "I give you my promise." And with these words they went away, and stayed no longer in the crypt. And the good man lingered not, but, having finished his task, he put on his garments, and went to take his pastime in the monastery.

THUS the time came and went until a short space thereafter it befell that the abbot summoned to him the man who was so compact of goodness. Now, when he heard that he was summoned, and that the abbot had asked for him, his heart was full of bitterness, for he knew not what he should say. "Alas," thought he, "now am I accused. Never shall I be for a day without annoy and travail and shame, for my service is as naught. I fear it is not pleasing to God, but rather, alas! it is displeasing to Him, since the truth of it has become known. Did I think that such labour as mine and such pastime were fit to please the Lord God? Nay, they could not please Him. Alas! I have done no good thing. Woe is me! what shall I do? Woe is me! what shall I say? Oh, Fair, Sweet Father, what will become of me? Now shall I be undone and brought to shame; now shall I be driven hence, and be made a butt of out there in the world that is so full of evil. Holy Mary, Sweet Lady, how is my mind bewildered! Where to turn for counsel I know not. Lady, come you to my counsel. Most Gracious God, now succour me!

Rest not, stay not, come, and your holy Mother thereto; in God's name come not without her. Come ye both to my succour, for in sooth I know not how to plead. They will say straightway and at the first word: 'Hence! get you gone!' Woe is me! what can I answer, I who know not a word to say? Alas, what avails it? Go hence I needs must." Weeping, so that his face was wet with his tears, he came before the abbot; weeping, he kneeled down before him. "My lord," he said, "mercy, in God's name. Would you drive me out from here? Say what you command of me, and I will do all your bidding."

31

HEN the abbot said: "I would know concerning you, and I would that you should tell me the truth. You have been here for a long time, year in and year out, and I would know in what manner you serve, and how you earn your bread." "Alas," said he, "well knew I that when my labours became known I should straightway be driven forth, and the folk here would have no more to do with me. I will go my way, my lord," he said. "Wretched I am, and wretched I shall be, and of good I never did any whit." The abbot answered: "I do not say that. But I beg and entreat, and thereto I command you in virtue of obedience, that you open your heart to me, and tell me by what trade you serve us here in our monastery." "My lord," returned the other, "you take my life, for your command is as death to me." Then he told him, howsoever great was his grief, all the story of his life from end to end, and left not a word unsaid, but told it all in one telling, just as I have told it to you. He said and related it all to him, weeping and with clasped hands; and, sighing, he kissed his feet.

The holy abbot came to him, and, weeping, he raised him up. He kissed him on both his eyes. "Brother," he said, "now say no more, for I pledge you my word that you shall be of our fellowship. God grant that we may be so deserving in our own as to be of yours! And you and I will be good friends. Fair, sweet brother, pray for me, and I will pray for you. And I beg you, sweet friend, and command you in all sincerity that you perform your service even as you have done hitherto, and yet more diligently if you are able." "My lord," he asked, "is this said in very truth?" "In very truth," returned the abbot. And that he might be no more in doubt, he laid a penance upon him, whereat the good man was so rejoiced that, as the story says, he scarce knew what befell. 34

E must needs sit him down, and he turned all pale; and when his heart came back to him, his body was so rudely shaken by joy that a malady fell upon him, whereof he shortly died. But he did his office right cheerfully, and without rest, morning and evening, day and night, so that he missed not a single hour until he fell sick.

OW, in sooth, the sickness that held him was so great that he might not stir from his bed. And he was in grievous trouble for that he could not pay his dues; and this it was that tormented him most, for he complained no whit of his sickness, save that he feared

35

much lest he lose his penance, since he might no longer perform such labour as he had been wont to do. It seemed to him that he was all too slothful; and the good man, who was very simple, prayed God to receive him before he were undone by idleness. For he was in such sore distress, in that his affair had become known, that his heart might not endure it, and he must perforce lie still and might not stir. The holy abbot did him much honour, for he and his monks came every hour and sang before the bed. And the good man took such delight in what they sang to him of God that, if one had offered him the whole of Poitou in exchange therefor, he would not have taken it, such joy had he in hearing. He confessed and was penitent, and yet he doubted somewhat fearfully concerning himself. But what need of more? In the end death came to him.

THE abbot and all his monks were there, and many a priest and many a canon; they stood humbly watching the good man, and they saw all clearly a wondrous miracle. For they all saw with their own eyes that when he was about to die the Mother of God and the angels and the archangels came about him. And on the other side were the devils and the imps and the furies, — this is no fable. But the fiends crowded about him, and waited and watched in vain, for they were to have no part in his soul. For even as the soul left the body, and before it had time to fall, it was received by the Mother of God. And the holy angels who were there go their way singing for joy, and carry him to heaven as was decreed. And this was seen by the whole brotherhood, and by all the others who were there. Now they all knew and understood that God would no longer hide His love for His servant, but would that all should know and recognise the man's goodness. And much they mar-

velled, and much they rejoiced
thereat. They did him great honour, and bore him into their
church, where they performed
the divine office in noble wise.
And there was not one who did
not either sing or read in the
choir of the great church.

THEY buried him with
great honour, and looked
on him as a saint. And
then fairly and openly
the abbot told them all the adventure of the good man, and
of his way of life, even as you
have heard it, and of all he himself had seen in the crypt. And
the convent listened gladly. "In
sooth," said they, "it is good to
believe; and none should doubt

you concerning this thing, for truth bears witness to it. The matter is well proved at need; and henceforth must there be no doubt but that he has done his penance." Great joy had they among themselves thereat.

THUS the minstrel came to his end. He tumbled well, and served well; for thereby won he great honour such that no other may compare therewith. The holy fathers tell us that thus it befell this minstrel. And now let us pray to God, who is above all, that He grant us to serve Him so well that we may deserve His love.

Here ends the story of Our Lady's Tumbler.

40

This edition of OUR LADY'S TUMBLER is printed by John Wilson and Son of Cambridge during February, 1898, for Copeland and Day, Boston.

www.ingramcontent.com/pod-product-compliance
Lightning Source LLC
Chambersburg PA
CBHW030900260626
47169CB00008B/2619